An Incredible Case of

Other books by Kenneth Oppel

Barnes and the Brains Series:
A Bad Case of Ghosts
A Strange Case of Magic
A Crazy Case of Robots
An Incredible Case of Dinosaurs
*A Weird Case of Super-Goo**
Emma's Emu
Silverwing
Sunwing
The Live-Forever Machine
Dead Water Zone
Peg and the Whale
Follow that Star

* forthcoming

An Incredible Case of

DINOSAURS

KENNETH OPPEL

Illustrated by
Sam Sisco

Scholastic Canada Ltd.

Scholastic Canada Ltd.
175 Hillmount Rd., Markham, Ontario, Canada L6C 1Z7

Scholastic Inc.
555 Broadway, New York, NY 10012, USA

Scholastic Australia Pty Limited
PO Box 579, Gosford, NSW 2250, Australia

Scholastic New Zealand Ltd.
Private Bag 94407, Greenmount, Auckland,
New Zealand

Scholastic Publications Ltd.
Villiers House, Clarendon Avenue, Leamington Spa,
Warwickshire CV32 5PR, UK

Canadian Cataloguing in Publication Data

Oppel, Kenneth
    An incredible case of dinosaurs

(Barnes and the brains)
ISBN 0-439-98792-X

I. Sisco, Sam. II. Title. III. Series: Oppel, Kenneth. Barnes and the brains.

PS8579.P64I52 2001   jC813'.54   C2001-930184-7
PZ7.O66In 2001

6 5 4 3 2   Printed in Canada   2 3 4 5/0

For Philippa.

Contents

Chapter 1

Splish Splash

GILES SETTLED BACK in the bathtub with a contented sigh.

He had just managed to work up a thick bubbly foam on the water's surface, when the bathroom door suddenly flew open. Tina and Kevin Quark walked straight in and stood at the edge of the tub, looking down at him expectantly. Giles could only stare back at them, speechless. "Knocking," he managed to say. "Ever heard of it?"

"We have secured another commission," said Tina grandly.

"We've got a job," added Kevin.

"Kevin," said Tina with a weary sigh, "that's what I just said."

"Could have fooled me."

Giles slid down lower in the tub, the water lapping against his chin. Life had seemed so simple before he had met Tina and Kevin. Now that he'd been made a full partner in their genius business, it seemed he never had a moment's peace. Just last week, they'd been hired to deal with the Walshes' missing garden gnomes, and the Angelinis' creaking hinges. Then there had been a particularly nasty case involving a radio that only picked up country and western music. It didn't matter where the tuning needle was, or whether the radio was on or off — the same mournful singing and guitar strumming blared from the speakers.

Giles supposed he should feel grateful that business was going full blast. After all, he'd almost saved up enough for the remote-controlled airplane he'd had his eye on for months. But he couldn't help wishing things would slow down just a little.

"Here I am, just trying to enjoy a simple bath," he said to Tina and Kevin, "and in you come like *The Ride of the Valkyries*!"

"Ride of the *what*?" said Kevin.

"Barnes is saying we just barged in," Tina explained.

"Well, I guess we did," said Kevin good-naturedly. "Sorry about that, Barnes."

"Oh no, not at all!" he said. "Look, just climb right in, both of you!"

"Thank you, Barnes," said Tina, "but we're in a hurry. Maybe some other time."

"It was a joke," said Giles, rolling his eyes. "So, what's this new job?"

"A Miss Frost telephoned," said Tina, taking a small notebook from her pocket. "She says there's a problem with her swimming pool."

"What kind of problem?"

"How much do you know about underwater life forms, Barnes?"

"You know," said Kevin helpfully, "squiggly things with tentacles and suckers the size of — "

"In her swimming pool?" said Giles, glancing

nervously at the bathwater. "You must be joking!"

"All I know," said Tina calmly, "is that Miss Frost seems to think she has something strange living in her pool. I personally doubt very much that this is the case, but we'll need to make a full investigation tomorrow morning."

"Fine," said Giles. "Now if you'll both excuse me, I'm going to pull the plug."

Chapter 2

Prehistoric Glurp

THE BIG DOOR swung slowly open.

"Mr. Frost?" said Giles uncertainly.

"No," replied the man in the three-piece suit, "I'm Swift, Miss Frost's personal assistant. You must be the Quark geniuses. Miss Frost has been expecting you. Please come in."

It was like a museum inside. Giles looked around the grand hallway in amazement. There were Roman sculpures on columns, ancient tapestries and paintings hanging from the walls, and ornate rugs covering the floor.

"An exquisite collection of Dutch Old Masters,"

Tina commented, nodding at a row of paintings. "Miss Frost must be a woman of some distinction."

"Wow!" Kevin exclaimed. "Look at all this stuff! It must be worth a fortune!"

"It is," said the assistant, giving Kevin a disdainful look. "So please don't touch anything. Follow me."

As they passed the living room, Giles thought there was an oddly empty feel to the place. He could see now that there was a fine, dusty silt over all the antique furniture and beautiful ornaments. Old cobwebs trailed from the picture frames.

Swift led them up a swirling marble staircase, then down a long, dimly lit corridor which ended with a set of wide double doors.

"Miss Frost's office is through here," the assistant told them, turning the huge doorknob. "Go in, please."

It was the biggest room Giles had ever seen.

Blinds covered all the windows, casting slices of dusty light into the room. A whole wall was filled with television monitors, numbers scrolling across their screens at a dizzying rate. At the far end of the room was a huge desk, with a long row of telephones on top.

And behind the desk sat an elegant, middle-aged woman. She was very pale, as if she hadn't seen the sun for quite some time. At the moment she was talking into one of the telephones.

"What do you mean, he won't sell?" she demanded in a steel-cold voice. "There's nothing that can't be bought! Everything has its price. Offer half a million! That should do the trick!"

She slammed down the phone and looked up fiercely at Giles, Kevin and Tina.

"So," she said, "you're the Quark geniuses."

"Well, they are," stammered Giles, pointing to Tina and Kevin.

"What are you, then?" asked Miss Frost with a scowl.

"I'm Giles Barnes."

"Not a genius yourself, young man?"

"I'm afraid not, no," replied Giles awkwardly.

"What a shame."

At that moment, all the telephones on her desk went off like a bomb.

"Buy!" she barked into the first phone.

"Sell!" she yelled into the second.

"Tell her if she pulls out we'll sue!" she roared into a third.

Giles swallowed hard.

"All right, then," said Miss Frost calmly, "where were we?"

Tina cleared her throat and opened her notebook.

"Miss Frost, I can see you're very busy, so we'll try to take as little of your time as possible. Perhaps you could tell us more about your swimming pool problem."

"It's obvious to me that something is living in it," she said matter-of-factly. "I'm not talking about ducks or geese or swans. Twice this past week, I've seen some sort of strange creature break the surface of the water, float on top for a moment, then dive back down again."

"What did this creature look like?" Tina asked.

"I've only seen it at night from the window," Miss Frost replied, "so I didn't get a very good look. But it reminded me of a giant jellyfish, or a squid."

Kevin looked over at Giles and smiled weakly. Tina was busily taking notes.

"And there have been noises," Miss Frost went on. "A kind of gurgling moan."

"A gurgling moan?" squeaked Kevin.

"Yes."

"Have you ever seen it swimming around in day-light?" Giles asked.

"It's not that simple," she replied. "It's a very large pool, and it's in very poor shape. I've simply been too busy to keep it up and — well, you'll see what I mean soon enough."

"What would you like us to do, exactly?" Giles asked.

"I want a full investigation," said Miss Frost. "I want a comprehensive report. I want to know if what I've seen is truly some strange creature, or a figment of my imagination. And, of course," she added, raising a pale finger in the air, "I insist that you keep this matter strictly secret. I don't want any of this spreading around, not even to your parents. Rumours start so quickly, and I wouldn't want people to think I was — "

"A complete loony?" Kevin suggested helpfully. Then he looked down at his feet, his face flushing bright red.

"You'll have to excuse my brother, Miss Frost," said Tina. "Sadly, he wasn't blessed with as large a brain as my own. In fact, in numerous tests I've performed on him, it seems he really only has a very tiny brain."

"I see," said Miss Frost. "So it turns out I've hired one genius for the price of three."

"I think you'll find that my brain more than makes up for the others," said Tina with supreme confidence.

"I sincerely hope so," said Miss Frost. "Swift will show you to the pool now."

* * *

Swift was waiting for them outside Miss Frost's door, standing as still as a department-store mannequin. He made Giles's skin crawl. They were led back downstairs, then outside to a broad patio that was surrounded on all sides by a ferociously over-grown garden.

"Here we are," said the assistant.

Giles frowned. "Um, where's the swimming pool?"

"Here we are," Swift said again, looking straight ahead, hands clasped behind his back.

"I don't understand," Kevin said.

Swift sighed, picked up a small stone and threw it into a ragged patch of greenery.

Plok!

"There's water underneath all that?" said Giles, incredulous.

"As Miss Frost indicated, it's in rather poor repair," said the assistant, and with that he turned and marched away.

All three of them stood there in stunned silence.

Giles walked cautiously to the edge of the concrete patio for a better look. It was as if the entire garden had just grown right into the swimming pool. A thick carpet of green algae and lily pads covered the water, and strange-looking plants sprouted leafy tendrils across the surface.

"Look at all that glurp!" said Kevin.

"That's not a word, Kevin," Tina told him.

"I'd say glurp is a pretty good word for what

we're looking at," Giles said.

A big, oily bubble bulged on the water's surface and burst with a thick popping sound.

"It's like a prehistoric swamp!" he exclaimed. "How are we supposed to see what's in the pool?"

Tina turned thoughtfully to her brother.

"Kevin, how would you feel about stripping down and just having a little paddle around?"

"Forget it!" Kevin exclaimed.

"No, I didn't think so," said Tina regretfully.

"You really think there's some weird creature in there?" Giles said.

"Of course not," said Tina confidently. "I'm sure there's a perfectly reasonable explanation for what Miss Frost saw."

Another big bubble popped at the water's surface, and a gurgling moan welled up from the depths of the pool.

Giles looked nervously over at Kevin.

"Could have been the wind," Kevin said quickly.

"Well," said Tina, "there's only one way to find out. We'll have to go underwater with the bathysphere!"

"The bathysphere?" Giles said to Kevin.

"Don't even ask," Kevin replied wearily.

Chapter 3

Into the Deep

"IT LOOKS LIKE a washing machine!" Giles exclaimed.

Tina sighed long-sufferingly. "Barnes, even the greatest inventors are forced to work with the raw materials at hand. In this case, a washing machine happened to be most suitable starting point."

"Mom was not impressed," panted Kevin, who had single-handedly pushed the huge contraption from home. He was lying flat on his back on Miss Frost's patio, catching his breath.

"We can't go underwater in this thing!" Giles said. "Look at it! There are still dials on top that say RINSE and SPIN CYCLE!"

"I don't think either of you fully appreciates the greatness of my latest invention," Tina said haughtily. "This bathysphere is capable of going underwater to great depths, while safely carrying three people inside. It will allow us to make a thorough aquatic examination of the pool."

Giles walked slowly around the bathysphere, taking a good look. Tina had certainly made a lot of alterations. At the rear was a huge propeller that looked suspiciously like the ceiling fan in the Quarks' dining room. Four bicycle lights had been bolted to the front. On either side of the bathysphere were bolted big oil drums, which sounded hollow when Giles tapped them. Thick rubber hosing was wrapped all around the outside, and truck tires were nailed to the base. It was much bigger than a regular washing machine. Giles peered through the round glass hatch. Still, it looked like a tight squeeze in there.

"I'm not sure about this," Giles said.

"It's perfectly safe, Barnes," Tina said. "I've tested it extensively."

"That's what you said about the turbo toaster," Kevin reminded her. "Dad nearly lost an eye." He turned to Giles. "That toast came out of there like a rocket!"

"Fine," said Tina, "I'll go alone. All the more glory for me, making the first descent all by myself — "

"All right, all right," sighed Giles. After all, she *was* a genius. "We're coming."

He helped Kevin to his feet and together they rolled the bathysphere off the deck and into the swampy water. It rode high on the surface, buoyed by the rubber tires and oil drums.

Tina opened the round glass hatch.

"Everyone in," she said.

It was a tight squeeze. Giles thought the inside looked like an airplane cockpit, with switches, gauges and buttons on all sides and overhead, too. He found it all kind of reassuring. Something with this many switches had to work.

Tina clanged the hatch shut behind her and sat at the controls between Giles and Kevin.

"Beginning descent!" she said, pushing buttons and throwing levers.

The bathysphere was slowly sinking. Giles watched as the gurgling water crept higher and higher up the round glass window. Soon it was level with his face, and he could see half below and half above the water. He caught himself holding his breath as the bathysphere sank completely under the surface.

It had become very dark all of a sudden, and Tina flipped another switch. The bicycle lights came on, and the water glowed eerily all around them.

Giles could hardly believe they were in a swimming pool. It certainly didn't look like one.

It was another world, murky green and vast. There was no sign of any walls. Far below them, the pool bottom was so covered in dirt and stones that it looked like the ocean floor. Fat gas bubbles wobbled past them towards the surface. A school of rainbow-coloured fish flitted across their path.

"Hey, how did they get in here?" Kevin asked.

"There must be another way into this pool," Tina said solemnly.

She steered the bathysphere deeper along the bottom.

"Look at that!" said Giles, pointing.

Lying toppled along the bottom was a huge statue of Poseidon.

"It must have fallen in from the patio," said Kevin. "Wow. It's like the lost continent of Atlantis down here!"

"Never mind that," said Tina, "I think I've found something interesting."

She aimed the lights at a long, jagged crack in the pool floor, near the statue. The crack was wide — about half a metre, Giles guessed.

"There must be an underground river below," said Tina. "Or else all the water would have drained through that crack. Let's have a closer look."

"Gork!" said Kevin suddenly.

"Sorry, I didn't quite get that, Kevin," Tina said.

"Thlurk!" Kevin managed to say.

Giles looked over to see Kevin pointing out the window with a trembling hand, his eyes huge.

"Th . . . th . . . there's something moving over there."

"Are you sure?" asked Tina.

Kevin nodded.

Tina jiggled a few switches and the beams of light swept around.

"I don't see anything," said Giles. "What did it look like, Kevin?"

"Big. Big and floppy."

"Big and floppy," said Tina, shaking her head with a sigh. "Very scientific, Kevin. Thank you."

"Big and floppy and kind of green."

"Oh, terrific," said Tina sarcastically.

Suddenly, something smacked against the bathysphere window.

Something big and floppy, and definitely green.

"That's it!" wailed Kevin. "That's what I saw!"

It was gone so quickly, Giles didn't even have time to focus on it.

"Let's surface!" said Kevin. "This isn't fun any-more!"

"Certainly not!" said Tina. "Not when we've just made visual contact!"

"There it is again!" said Giles.

"Don't go too close," said Kevin, his voice shaky.

Tina aimed the spotlight at the creature. She sighed.

"So this is it, huh? Big and floppy and green."

It was a tattered tarpaulin, floating just off the bottom of the pool, its ratty edges undulating like tentacles.

"It looked so much bigger when I saw it," Kevin said sheepishly.

"This must be Miss Frost's creature," said Giles with relief.

"Yes," said Tina wisely. "A gas bubble must lift the tarp up through the water. At the top, all the gas escapes, and the tarp sinks back down to the bottom. It could keep going up and down like that forever."

"Well," said Kevin, who had cheered up considerably, "that's another case cracked by the Quark genius business." He nudged Giles. "See, it wasn't worth getting so scared about, was it?"

Something nudged up against the bathysphere window, blotting out the light.

"Gork!" said Kevin again.

Giles knew exactly what he meant this time.

This wasn't a tarpaulin.

This was something else.

This something had a purple, wedge-shaped head with green-rimmed eyes, and a long, narrow mouth lined with two sharp mountain ranges of teeth!

Chapter 4

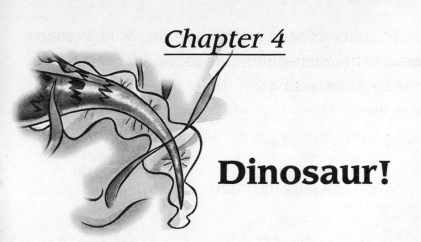

Dinosaur!

MISS FROST LOOKED UP as they burst into her office.

"You've got something, all right!" Kevin blurted out, skidding across the floor.

"A creature!" said Giles. "There is definitely a strange creature living in your pool!"

"I see," Miss Frost replied calmly. "You're quite sure about that, are you?"

"Sure?" said Kevin. "You should have seen the teeth on that thing!"

"Thank you, Kevin," said Tina firmly, "that will be enough. Miss Frost, I'm pleased to report that I have made visual contact with the creature in question, and have managed to make an identification."

"Go on," she said.

"Unless I'm mistaken," Tina began, "and I so rarely am, the creature is actually a very rare species of *Hydrosaurus*."

"Are you telling me I have a dinosaur living in my pool?"

"Yes I am, Miss Frost."

Giles had never seen anyone take such extraordinary news so calmly.

"How did it get there?"

"Through a crack in the bottom," said Giles. "It must swim in from some underground river. After we saw it, it darted back down through the crack."

A telephone rang. Miss Frost picked it up, said, "Not now," and hung up.

She looked back at the three of them and smiled. "Excellent. A remarkable job."

"Well, I think that about wraps things up here," said Kevin eagerly. "It's been a real pleasure, Miss Frost. We'll send you our bill and — "

"No, no," said Miss Frost. "You're not finished yet."

"We're not?" said Giles.

"I wonder how much a dinosaur is worth?" Miss Frost said quietly, turning towards the flashing wall of television screens. "It's one of a kind. I'd be the only person in the world to have one." She looked sternly at the three of them. "I want you to catch it for me."

"Catch it?" exclaimed Kevin.

"Miss Frost," said Giles, "catching hydrosaurs really isn't the kind of thing we do."

"It isn't at all," agreed Kevin. "I mean, the last time we caught dinosaurs was — "

"I want that hydrosaur," said Miss Frost in her steely voice.

"I'm sure we could trap it for you," said Tina confidently.

Giles stared at her in amazement.

"But — " he began to say.

"But — " Kevin began to say.

"Good!" said Miss Frost. "That's the kind of attitude I like in my business."

She opened a drawer and took out the thickest wallet Giles had ever seen.

"And rest assured," she said, "I'll make it very worth your while."

* * *

"I can't believe we're actually trying to catch a dinosaur," said Giles nervously.

"It's a scientific breakthrough," said Tina grandly. "Think about it, Barnes. Until now, all we've had to go on are dinosaur bones. But now we've discovered a living specimen! It might be millions of years old! Or this particular species might never have died out at all! It's absolutely essential we catch it!"

"Besides," added Kevin, "did you see the size of Miss Frost's wallet? We're going to be rich!"

They had been waiting in the bathysphere for a long time now — hovering at the bottom of the pool, near the large crack. But so far there had been no sign of the hydrosaur.

"I don't understand why the dinosaur keeps coming back here anyway," said Giles.

"After we catch it," said Tina, flipping some switches, "and I have time to study it properly, perhaps I'll have an answer to that question."

"I just hope this plan of yours works," said Giles dubiously.

All at once, the dinosaur slipped up through the crack and circled gracefully through the water. For the first time, Giles got a good look at it. Its skin was a deep purple, with brilliant streaks of green. Its body was quite slender, with four leathery fins jutting out from its sides. It had a very long, very thin neck, which ended with its small, wedge-shaped head.

"Look at it move!" said Giles in awe. "It's so fast!"

"Here we go!" said Tina excitedly. She edged the bathysphere forward until it nudged against the huge statue of Poseidon. The propeller whirred loudly, and the whole vessel began to shudder.

"The statue's too big!" shouted Giles.

"It won't budge!" cried Kevin.

"We have the power!" said Tina through gritted teeth.

The propeller's whining increased in pitch, and the bathysphere shook so violently that Giles thought it would burst apart at any moment. But slowly, the statue of Poseidon began to scrape

across the pool floor, towards the long crack.

"It's working!" said Tina.

A second hydrosaur suddenly darted up through the opening — this one a bright yellow, with a pink underbelly. The two dinosaurs rolled playfully through the water together.

"Look!" gasped Giles. "We've got two now!"

"We've got an incredible case of dinosaurs!" said Kevin.

Tina threw another lever and the bathysphere pushed ahead some more. In a few seconds, the statue rolled into place over the crack, blocking the opening completely.

"Miss Frost," Tina said with satisfaction, "is now the proud owner of two dinosaurs."

Chapter 5

Smarter Than You Think

GILES WRINKLED HIS NOSE as he plunged his hand into the bucket, grabbed another fish and threw it into the pool. One of the dinosaurs snapped it up before it even hit the water.

"They sure do eat a lot," said Kevin, lobbing a cod tail to the other hydrosaur.

"Good job, you two," said Tina. "Keep it up." She was stretched out in a lawn chair at the poolside, a micro-cassette recorder in one hand, a glass of iced tea in the other. Every so often she would lift the cassette recorder to her face, speak into it, then smile and shake her head with a small chuckle — as if what she'd just said was the most amusing and remarkable thing she'd ever heard.

Giles rolled his eyes in disgust.

"I don't suppose you want to take a turn feeding them?" he asked.

"No need to be sarcastic, Barnes," Tina replied. "Anyone can see I'm extremely busy making scientific notes on these specimens."

"Right," Giles grumbled.

Every day after school, for the past week, he and Kevin had made the trip to the local fish market to buy pounds and pounds of raw fish for the hydrosaurs. The bus driver refused to let them on with their stinking buckets of dinosaur food, so they had to lug them all the way to Miss Frost's house by foot. People on the street would sniff, then stop, then sniff again, then stare as they passed by. It was the worst!

"This is going to make headlines," Tina said contentedly. " 'Local genius discovers dinosaurs.' Or maybe, 'Breakthrough of century made by local genius.' Or what about 'Tina Quark wins Nobel Prize'? It's been far too long since I was on the front page of a newspaper."

"At least you're not the one who goes home every day smelling like a barnacle," Giles told her.

"You've got nothing to complain about, Barnes," Tina said. "Miss Frost is paying us all very generously to take care of the dinosaurs. A few more days and you'll have enough for that remote-controlled airplane you've wanted for so long. Don't you want to be rich?"

Giles sighed. He supposed he did want to be rich. After all, who didn't? And he definitely wanted that airplane. Yesterday he'd passed the store window where it was displayed. He was always a little afraid that the next time it would be gone. Soon, though, he'd be able to walk right into the store, put his money down on the counter, and take the airplane home himself.

But he felt uneasy. And it wasn't just because he had to heft buckets of smelly fish around every day. He looked at the two hydrosaurs in the pool.

"I don't think they're very happy, trapped like that," he told Tina.

"Don't be ridiculous, Barnes," said Tina. "They

have brains the size of grape seeds. Would you feel sorry for a goldfish in a bowl? I don't think so. These creatures probably don't even realize they're trapped!"

But Giles wasn't so sure. After they'd rolled the statue of Poseidon over the crack, the two hydro-saurs had prodded at it with their heads, and darted back and forth in confusion. And a ghostly moaning had drifted through the water. It was the most mournful thing Giles had ever heard.

And Giles thought they looked a little listless sometimes, floating near the surface, their wedge-shaped heads peering out at him. At other times they seemed restless, churning the swampy water into a froth as they tore around the perimeter of the pool, faster and faster, as if they were desperate to escape.

"How do you know they're so stupid?" Giles asked.

"Everyone knows the dinosaurs weren't very bright," Tina replied wisely. "All these creatures can do is swim and eat. They're savage beasts. They're eating machines."

"I wonder what Miss Frost is going to do with them?" Giles wondered aloud.

It wasn't as if she'd taken any real interest in the dinosaurs. She hadn't even come down to the poolside to have a close look. A few times, Giles had turned to see her watching from her office window, but, once spotted, she always quickly disappeared from sight. What a strange person she was, Giles thought, working all alone in that huge house, with only her creepy personal assistant, Swift, for company!

"I want to get a shot of the dinosaurs," said Kevin, taking a camera from his backpack. "Barnes, can you stand by the edge, holding a fish?"

"Do I have to?"

"Yeah. It'll be a great photo."

Giles faced Kevin, holding a fish head as far away from his body as possible.

"A little further back, Barnes. You're not in the picture."

He took another step back.

"A little more! There's plenty of room!"

Another few steps.

"Um, Barnes . . . " he heard Kevin say suddenly.

The next thing he knew, he was deep in the pool, swampy water shooting up his nostrils. Spluttering, he fought to get back to the surface, but his clothes were drenched and dragging him down. His head popped up for a moment, but he just managed to suck in a breath of air before sinking under again.

I'm a goner! he thought in pure panic. I'm about to get eaten by dinosaurs!

Opening his eyes, he made out a blurry purple shape swirling around him, and then felt it brush past him. This is it, he thought, gritting his teeth. Here it comes. He felt the dinosaur nudge its head against his backside and then push hard. Giles was propelled up and out of the water, as if he were in an ejector seat! He sailed through the air and landed at the edge of the pool, dripping water, still spluttering.

"Wow!" gasped Kevin.

"Extraordinary!" said Tina, who had put down her glass of iced tea and was standing at the poolside with Kevin.

"Am I ever sorry, Barnes!" said Kevin worriedly, slapping him on the back. "I had no idea you were so close to the edge! I was about to dive in and save you!"

"You most definitely were not, Kevin," said Tina witheringly.

"Well, I was planning on doing something!" Kevin said. "Are you okay, Barnes?"

Giles nodded. He still felt a little shaky. He could see the dinosaur poking its head above the water, watching him with its bright eyes.

"It didn't eat me!" he stammered. "It lifted me out!"

He'd heard all sorts of stories about shipwrecked sailors being saved from drowning by dolphins. He'd just been saved by a hydrosaur!

"They must be smarter than you think, Tina," Kevin told his sister.

"And friendlier," Giles said.

"And much cuddlier than I first thought," added Kevin, waving at the purple dinosaur in the pool.

Tina frowned. Then she stalked back to her lawn chair and started muttering into her cassette recorder.

Chapter 6

The Big Deal

GILES LOOKED at the remote-controlled airplane in the store window.

"It's a beauty, all right," Kevin said.

Giles crinkled the money in his pocket. He'd waited a long time for this airplane — and now, thanks to their dinosaur job, he could finally buy it. He knew every detail of the airplane by now, and had often daydreamed about taking it on its first flight in the big field near his house.

"It's great being rich, isn't it?" said Kevin cheerfully. "Now I can buy a radio to replace the one Tina blew up last month. Those dinosaurs are the best thing that's ever happened to the genius business!"

Giles jammed his hands into his pockets and turned away from the window.

"Aren't you going to buy it?" Kevin asked in confusion.

"We've got to set them free," Giles said.

"What? The dinosaurs?"

"It's not fair to keep them trapped in that pool," said Giles. "And all because Miss Frost wants to own the only dinosaurs in the world! It's like all those other valuable things in her house just collecting dust! It's just greedy!"

How could he possibly buy the airplane with the money Miss Frost had given him? He knew he'd feel too guilty.

"Do you really think they mind staying in the pool?" Kevin asked with a frown.

"How would you like it if someone boxed *you* in?"

"Tina was thinking about it once," Kevin replied thoughtfully, "but I managed to talk her out of it. You're right, Barnes, I don't think it would be very comfortable at all."

"They're not eating as much as they used to, either," Giles said. "They're definitely unhappy. We should set them free."

Kevin shook his head uncertainly.

"Tina won't like it," he said. "Do you know what she's doing right now? She's at home, dictating her memoirs! Once I passed her door and heard her practising some kind of acceptance speech. She kept saying things like 'Thank you for this great honour' and 'I knew it was only a matter of time before my great genius was recognized by the international community.' She's counting on these dinosaurs, Barnes. She thinks they're going to make her world-famous!"

"We'll have to do it without telling her."

"But what about Miss Frost? She's not going to let us set them free. She owns the dinosaurs! And you've heard the way she talks to people on the phone! She's tough, Barnes. She's downright scary! There's no way we'll ever convince her!"

"There's only one way," said Giles. "We've got to make her a deal."

* * *

Swift opened the door, blinked and stared in amazement.

On the doorstep stood Giles and Kevin, both dressed in large, dark suits and ties borrowed from Mr. Barnes's closet. Kevin wore sunglasses and a scowl. His hair was slicked back with half a bottle of hair gel, and his arms were folded menacingly across his chest. Giles held a briefcase in one hand.

"We're here to see Miss Frost," he said.

Without waiting for a reply, he and Kevin marched through the door and headed for the curving marble staircase.

"Wait! You can't just barge in here!" Swift objected, hurrying to block their way. "Miss Frost is far too busy to be bothered by unannounced visitors."

"Move aside, sir," said Kevin in a very deep, very serious voice. "We don't want anyone getting hurt."

Swift stepped back without hesitation. Giles was impressed.

They made their way quickly up the stairs. Kevin — practically blind in his sunglasses — had to feel his way along the banister to avoid tripping.

Miss Frost was on the telephone when they burst into her office.

"I'll make him an offer he can't refuse!" she growled. Snatching up another phone, she said, "Tell him he'd better sell now, or he'll be eating potatoes for the rest of his life!"

Giles gulped.

Maybe this wasn't such a good idea after all. But it was too late now. Miss Frost had caught sight of them and was frowning curiously.

"I'll call you back in thirty seconds," she said into the phone.

Giles took a deep breath, handed his briefcase to Kevin, and strode up to the huge desk.

"Miss Frost," he said, trying to sound firm and professional, "I have a deal for you."

"Is that Giles Barnes?"

"That's correct."

"And who is this with you?"

"This is my personal assistant."

"How did you get his hair to do that?"

"Never mind that right now, Miss Frost."

"Why is he wearing sunglasses?"

"To look menacing," Kevin said helpfully.

Miss Frost glanced at her day planner.

"I don't believe we have an appointment today," she said.

"No, we don't," said Giles brusquely. "But this simply couldn't wait."

"Oh?"

"I want to buy those dinosaurs, Miss Frost, and I'm prepared to make you a cash offer right now."

Giles thought he saw a sparkle of admiration in her eyes.

"Go on," she said.

Giles suddenly drew a blank. He simply didn't know what to say next. Instead, he snapped his fingers. Kevin stepped forward obediently and helped him off with his jacket, draping it over his arm. Giles cleared his throat and adjusted his tie. He had no idea what he was doing, but it all seemed incredibly professional. For good measure he snapped his fingers again and Kevin stepped forward with the jacket and helped Giles back into it.

He felt much better now.

"Let me be candid, Miss Frost. Allow me to get

straight to the heart of the matter. I'm not a man to mince words. Speaking as one businessperson to another, I think we can hammer out a deal that is mutually beneficial."

He hadn't the slightest idea where all these words were coming from, but they were pouring into his mind thick and fast.

"I think you'll find that my offer speaks for itself."

He snapped his fingers again, and Kevin brought over the briefcase and set it on Miss Frost's desk. Giles gave a curt nod. Kevin opened the clasps and flipped up the top. Inside was a small, rumpled stack of money, held together by an elastic band. Scattered across the bottom of the briefcase was an assortment of coins.

Miss Frost carefully counted the money. Giles looked over at Kevin and smiled weakly. Would it be enough? He didn't think it looked nearly as impressive as it had earlier in his bedroom. But it was all the money he'd saved up for the remote-controlled airplane, plus some of Kevin's savings from the genius business.

"You realize, of course," said Miss Frost, "that these dinosaurs are worth over a million times the amount you have here."

Giles instantly felt ridiculous.

"Really?"

"I'm afraid so, yes."

"Well," said Giles, "this is all I have."

Miss Frost looked at him curiously.

"And you're willing to spend all of it on the dinosaurs?"

Giles nodded firmly. "It's just money."

Miss Frost gazed thoughtfully at all the television screens flashing numbers, then turned towards the windows.

"What did you want to do with these dinosaurs?"

"Set them free."

"But why?" she asked in amazement.

"They're sad and restless. They're big animals, and much smarter than you might think. And it can't be very comfortable for them, being crammed into the swimming pool."

"No," said Miss Frost, "I guess not."

She looked back at the money in the briefcase with a small smile.

She's going to say no, thought Giles glumly. So much for that idea. All he'd done was make a fool of himself. He should have known she'd never go for it.

"This," said Miss Frost, looking up at Giles, "is the best deal that's ever been offered to me."

Giles gaped.

Kevin's sunglasses fell off his face.

"Are you serious?" Giles exclaimed.

"I am," replied Miss Frost. "You drive a hard bargain, Giles, but you've got yourself a deal. I only wish I could take a good, close look at those dinosaurs before they go."

"But why can't you?" Giles asked, confused. He thought of her secretly watching from the window. Why hadn't she ever just come down to the pool?

"I can't possibly leave my office," she explained. "I might miss an important phone call."

"Wouldn't they call back?" Kevin asked.

"Or I might miss a blip on one of the monitors," she said, waving her hand at the wall of flashing screens.

"A blip?" said Kevin. "Is that serious?"

"It could be," she replied. "It could be very serious. It depends on what kind of blip we're talking about. It might be a zig or a zag."

"A zig or a zag?" said Giles.

"That would be quite serious."

"I see," said Kevin.

"But not as serious as a dip," she went on. "It would be disastrous if I missed a dip. Or a peak, or a trough, a swing, a boom or a bust — "

Suddenly she started to laugh.

"It sounds so ridiculous, doesn't it?" she said. "I stay trapped in this room, year after year, watching screens and shouting into phones. It's ridiculous! I'm coming out to see the dinosaurs!"

"Great!" said Giles.

Miss Frost stood up. She walked out from behind her desk.

The three of them had almost reached the door when the phone rang.

Oh, no, Giles thought.

Miss Frost hesitated. She looked at the ringing phone, then back at Giles and Kevin.

"It's only money, after all," she said with a smile, and then turned and walked out the door of her office.

Chapter 7

Hatched

"THEY'RE BEAUTIFUL!" exclaimed Miss Frost, peering at the dinosaurs through the bathysphere's glass hatch. "It's been far too long since I've taken the time to really look at things! Look at them move!"

Giles guided the bathysphere smoothly down to the bottom of the pool. He'd watched Tina enough times to know how to use the controls. The two hydrosaurs glided gracefully through the water around them.

"Did you ever figure out why they came in the first place?" Miss Frost asked.

Giles shook his head. "Not really. Tina thought that maybe they got lost on their way to the ocean."

In the distance, in the far corner of the pool, Giles made out a small mound of stones that he'd never noticed before.

"What's that?" he said, steering the bathysphere over for a closer look.

All at once the two dinosaurs cut in front of him, blocking his way. Again and again, they streaked anxiously past the hatch, making a low, gurgling moan.

"They don't want you to get any closer!" Kevin exclaimed.

"I wonder why?" said Miss Frost.

Giles squinted at the strange mound and caught a glimpse of something white nestled among the rocks.

Suddenly, everything made sense.

"Look! It's an egg!" Giles shouted. "That's why they came here. To make a nest. It's the perfect place for it, too. Safe and quiet!"

As they all watched, the egg began to shudder slightly.

"It's hatching!" said Kevin.

The two hydrosaurs swam in close and swirled around the egg. At first, Giles couldn't see what was going on. But after a few minutes, he managed to catch a glimpse of a small, bright red, wedge-shaped head, peeping out from the top of the cracked egg.

"Let's set them free now," said Miss Frost.

Giles turned the bathysphere around and pushed up against the huge statue of Poseidon. He opened up the throttle to full, and the propeller whirred furiously. Gradually, the statue scraped across the pool floor until the crack was completely uncovered.

The dinosaurs didn't waste a second.

The first hydrosaur shot down through the opening like a flash of purple lightning. Then the red, baby hydrosaur swam a little clumsily towards the crack, nudged along by the pink dinosaur. After the baby wobbled down out of sight, the last hydrosaur circled magnificently around the bathysphere once, then darted into the fissure and was gone.

* * *

"I'm trying to remain calm," said Tina.

"That's good," said Kevin nervously. "Breathe deeply."

"I am breathing deeply, Kevin. I am breathing as deeply as I know how. If I breathe any deeper I am going to blow up like a balloon and POP!"

Kevin jumped.

"Barnes, do you have any idea what you've done?" Tina asked miserably.

"I think I'm about to find out," Giles replied.

"You've destroyed my career, Barnes. I'm finished. Ruined. Washed up. I spent the best days of my life studying those two dinosaurs. I was ready to make scientific history! They were the only two living dinosaurs ever seen by mankind."

"Three," Kevin reminded her good-naturedly. "Don't forget the baby hydrosaur."

"Thank you, Kevin," said Tina through clenched teeth. "Of course, I didn't get the chance to see the baby dinosaur, thanks to you both! Did you know I'd been invited to speak at the university? Did you know I'd practically finished my memoirs? *Tina Quark: A Brilliant Life*. It would have been a bestseller."

"Look on the bright side," said Kevin. "We got

another job for the genius business out of it. Miss Frost has hired us to clean up her house."

Tina shook her head dejectedly.

"From award-winning scientist to cleaning staff," said Tina. "This is a very sad day. I'm completely at a loss."

"I'm not," said Giles, stretching his arms above his head with a yawn. "I know exactly what I'm going to do. I'm going to go home and have a nice, relaxing bath. And, if it's all the same to you, I'd like to have it alone this time."

Kenneth Oppel's first book, *Colin's Fantastic Video Adventure,* was published when he was fifteen years old. Since then he has written sixteen more books, including the best-selling novels *Silverwing* and *Sunwing,* both of which have won the Mr. Christie's Book Award and the Canadian Library Association's Book of the Year for Children Award. Kenneth lives in Toronto with his wife and two children.

The first exciting
Barnes and the Brains adventure!

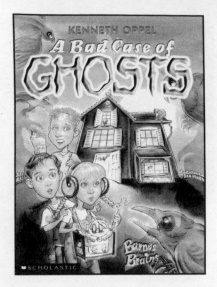

Giles Barnes and his family have just moved — into a very strange house. Creaks, rustles, and fluttering sounds fill his bedroom. His mother insists there is no such thing as ghosts, but Giles decides to investigate. He enlists the help of his new neighbours, "local geniuses" Tina and Kevin Quark, and their "ghostometer," and together Barnes and the Brains solve the mystery — and get rid of the ghosts for good!

A Bad Case of Ghosts
by Kenneth Oppel
ISBN 0-590-51750-3
$4.99

Barnes and the Brains,
back on the case!

When Giles, Tina and Kevin see books moving in the
library, all by themselves, they know they have to
investigate. But Tina's amazing ghostometer doesn't pick
up any ghosts, so what could that mysterious presence
be? Nobody expects what they actually find — and once
again, it takes a dose of Giles's own common-sense magic
to get things back to normal.

A Strange Case of Magic
by Kenneth Oppel
ISBN 0-439-98732-6
$4.99

More mayhem for Barnes and the Brains!

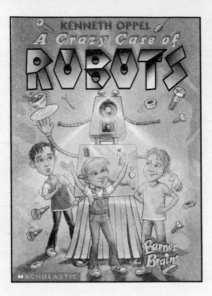

Tina Quark has invented the ultimate robot! The Tinatron 1000 is programmed to perform any task flawlessly — from cleaning to homework, and everything in between. When Tina asks Giles Barnes to robot-sit, the robot's perfect ways drive him perfectly crazy. And when Tinatron's circuits start to overload, sparks fly! Can Barnes and the Brains outsmart a renegade robot?

A Crazy Case of Robots
by Kenneth Oppel
ISBN 0-439-98824-1
$4.99